The

Bear's Last Word

(on the Matter)

by

Will Knight

PAPILLON DU PÈRE
PUBLISHING

This KINDLE 2nd edition compiled by

Papillon du Père Publishing

www.papillon-du-pere.com

CONTENTS

The Bear's Last Word (on the Matter)

"Would you like an adventure now," he said casually ...
"or would you like to have your tea first?"

– J.M. Barrie, *Peter Pan*

Now

James

A dvancing years beset each and everyone eventually, James knew, though he preferred to view the passage of time as experiences on his journey. Only, it wasn't his journey that was soon to reach its final destination. It was his friend's.

So perhaps now it was time to tell his story.

Flurries of snow flickered in the wind outside as he removed and dusted off his beanie, attending to it as one might a top hat at the ball. It was a gift last Christmas from his sister, Hayley. A pity she couldn't come today. His friend loved being doted on by her.

The building he'd entered was quite modern really; and quite warm—cozy even, he decided as he unbuttoned his winter wax jacket.

James sighed at what lay before him. One of his last visits to his childhood friend, no longer in rude health. Well, who likely is when they live in a care home? Yes, advancing years beset each and everyone. Not even his extraordinary childhood friend could overcome that.

Placing his beanie in his lower-left pocket, James blew into his hands, to warm them or to perhaps set himself for the task at hand. It would be bittersweet, but it might be fun, too, to remember the old days. Those days when he and his best buddy had lived all those adventures. Had *done* stuff. Stuff that didn't involve sitting at a computer, designing ... whatever he was asked in the brief.

Banks ... not exactly the most exciting clients. Which didn't exactly lend itself to being the most exciting life these days.

James looked up from wiping his feet on the mat. There she was, signaling him.

Now

Jess

She'd actually been the one to take the call in the office of the local newspaper. Well, it was her job, alongside being head reporter. And photocopier and coffeemaker. He had a story, maybe, he'd said. Might be good at Christmastime, he'd said. Be nice for kids to read about the main man.

"Main man?" she'd asked.

"Yeah, you know. Captain Christmas."

"Captain Christmas. As in … some new Marvel movie?"

The man chuckled. "Sorry, no. I mean the jolly fat guy that brings all the presents and things."

"Ah, Santa Claus."

"Yeah. Santa Claus."

Jess reached for her coffee cup, knocked it, and spilled its long-since-cold contents onto some papers. Oh well, nothing for it. She swept the liquid off with the arm of her sweater. Her *ridiculous* sweater. Who in their right mind would wear a sweater with such a crazy jolly fat guy in red on it? Reporters desperate for Holiday-season stories, that's who.

"Funny how folks always assume Santa is jolly at this time of year. I would have thought he'd be pretty stressed out every December," Jess said, wiping the excess liquid off her arm, the phone cricked into her neck.

"Well, he can be a bit," the man said. "But mostly he's pretty cool. And jolly."

"I see. And you'd know this how …?"

"I met him."

And now she sat in the waiting room of this care home, waiting for a surely ridiculous story. Her attention was caught by the movement of someone entering the building. That might be him. The young man who claimed to have lived fantastic adventures with a ... with a, well, a companion that defied belief.

Jess noted the man's reluctance to enter. She lifted a still damp arm and waved at him. She noticed a big smile spread across his face. A face that was round and appealing. Eyes that crinkled into the smile. And hair that refused to obey as he attempted to pat it down after removing his cap.

"Alright?" he said as he approached, his arm outstretched. "James Chapman."

"Jessica Walter. Pleased to meet you, Mr. Chapman."

"James, please. I don't want to get confused with my dad, Joseph."

His easy smile was warming. "Jess. Not to be confused with my mother, Mary, I hope."

James nodded.

"So ... look, I hope you don't mind ... I mean, I came mainly because the day was quiet. Not much going on right now. People are mainly interested in shopping and partying. No one actually does anything much else that's worth reporting on."

"That's fine. I wasn't going to call in. But if I don't do it now, then ... well, this is probably my last chance to. And it's cool if you don't believe my story. I'm not really doing it for you or anyone else. It's for my friend."

"Your ... *friend*."

"Yeah. Come on, I'll introduce you."

Now

James

James knocked gently on the door and opened it a crack. He peered in. The bed was empty, made neatly. Not by his friend, he doubted. No one changed from being so messy to being neat and tidy. At least, he hoped not.

He stuck his head inside the crack. And there he was on the sofa by the window, which resembled something of a wide cinema screen showing a nature documentary from Patagonia in winter. The snow danced behind his friend, who slowly and stiffly sat up and smiled.

Damn, he looks ... old. Even more so than when he'd visited last week.

"James!"

"Alright?"

Now

Jess

Jess followed James into the room.

What the ...?!

There he was, this special childhood friend. Just as James had claimed. Sitting on the sofa at the end of the smallish room was ... was a bear.

Unbelievably an actual *bear*. A little one. Maybe three feet tall? Round head, shaggy fur, gray as an old man's beard.

"Wh-what is this?" she stumbled out.

"My friend," James said. "Like I told you."

"But ... But h-he's a—"

"Bear, okay if we come in and chat?"

"Of course it is!"

Jess watched the bear take off a pair of half-lensed reading glasses and set his book aside. James moved easily inside and went to hug his friend, who struggled down—with a soft groan, she heard—from his sofa perch to stand on two ... paws ... to embrace his friend.

"What are you reading, mate?" James asked the little bear.

"Arabian Knights."

"Ah ... like the time we ..."

"Mm."

Jess watched them a moment before James turned around to her and said, "Come on in, Jess. Bear doesn't bite. Much."

Jess swallowed and let out the breath she'd been holding.

"Oi!" The bear playfully swiped at James's arm before struggling back onto the sofa, accepting a helping hand to do so. "I've never bitten anyone in my life! Only Penguins."

"Y-you eat penguins?!"

James laughed. "Only the chocolate ones. As many as he can get his hands on."

The bear smiled. "You didn't happen to ...?"

"Got some cake, yes."

"I want! Mmm ..."

Jess brushed a lock of auburn hair from her eye. "I-I ... Is this ... Are you ..."

"Real?" the bear finished.

"Well, um, yes."

The little bear lifted an arm and smelled his fur. "I stink, therefore I am."

Despite herself, Jess smiled at the bear's smile, writ large across his round head. Honestly, looking at him more closely now, if she had to describe the creature—and she would have to, of course—she'd say he looked like one of those bears off greetings cards.

The bear eagerly took one of the individual cakes James offered. He unwrapped it like a past master and broke a piece off. "Cake, Jess?"

"No, no, thank you. I don't usually accept treats from, um, bears. At least, not on a first meeting."

"Ah, I'm sure," the bear said, nodding. "Well, more for me! So, take your coat off. You can hang it over ... um ... gosh, where's that coat hook gone?"

"It's right over there, Bear," James said. "Here, Jess, let me hang that for you." James shed his own coat in an easy fluid motion and hung both on the hook in the opposite corner.

"Come sit beside me," the bear said. "Or ... opposite if you prefer?"

"Um ... yes, maybe over here is better."

"Ah, yes, of course. Put the kettle on, James? Fancy a cuppa, Jess?"

"You drink tea?"

"It's been known."

"Been known!" James snickered. "He used to insist on tea at teatime, on the dot, every day! Got to have your afternoon cuppa, eh, Bear!"

"The Turks call it *Keyif zahmanah.* It sort of comes to mean 'your time for you—something nice to enjoy.' I don't speak Turkish or anything. Not the modern version, anyway. More the old Ottoman ... from when we were there."

Jess shot him a glance.

Now

James

James stirred the pot of tea again and then poured it into three waiting mugs. "I see they've given you the Rudolph ones again this year, mate."

"Heat-change ones, James," Bear said. "Kind of cool. Or hot, I think I mean. Anyway ... Oh, thank you," he said, taking the mug James offered. "You didn't bring any cake or anything, did you?"

James watched as Bear took the mug gently but firmly, noting how much attention Bear now had to give to the task. "There's some right there, I see."

"Oh! Yummy."

Jess flipped open a notebook. And tapped a pen on the blank page. "I'm not sure where to start ... Maybe I could ask you where you came from ... Mr. Bear?"

"Just Bear. Don't want to be confused with my father." He winked.

James smiled and sipped his brew.

"An unusual name," Jess said.

Bear nodded and sipped his tea. "Blame him," he said, inclining his head to James.

"I, erm, lacked imagination in those days," James replied.

"Where did you come from, Bear?" Jess asked, her pen poised above the snow-white paper for the exposé.

"I dunno where I came from all those years ago. I just woke up one day. In James's bedroom."

James watched Jess scribble down a note. She looked up at him.

"Oh, sorry. Don't ask me. I was pretty young then. I just thought he was a cool Christmas present."

"Turns out this bear was for life, not just for Christmas, eh," Jess said.

James looked away. Not for life, no. He covered his reaction by sipping his tea.

"So ... I can't believe I'm going to ask this as a serious question, but given what—sorry, *who* is before me, I will. Tell me, did you really meet Santa Claus? *The* Santa Claus?

"Oh, yes! Of course. Twice, actually!" Bear said, his pride evident.

And why not? How many could say they had met Santa Claus?

"And what were the circumstances in which you both met him?"

"Ah," said Bear. "The first time—now *that's* a story, eh, James?"

James smiled widely. "It is."

"You should have listened to me! I told you we'd find trouble!"

"You were right, I admit it." They gently clinked mugs together.

"So ..." prompted Jess.

"So?" asked Bear.

"So tell me the story. I'd love to hear it."

"A story? You want a story, do you? James, let's tell her one of the Christmas adventures we had, shall we? We met Santa Claus, Jezz." Bear put his paw to the side of his nose. "Hush, hush. Don't tell anyone. Except for your readers, of course."

Jess looked at James, and he immediately got her unasked question. He nodded slightly, looked away. Bear was increasingly having problems holding onto the immediate present.

"We saved Christmas, Jess," Bear proclaimed. He broke off a piece of cake and put it nonchalantly into his mouth. Pleasure spread across his face.

James's heart winced. Just enjoy the time here and now, he told himself.

"That's quite an achievement, Bear," Jess said. "I'd love to hear more."

"We might need two pots for this," Bear said and sipped his tea. He looked at Jess and said, "Pen ready?"

"It is."

"Well, here goes. 'The elves were dead, to begin with ...'"

"Come again...?"

"Bear! Stop stealing from Dickens," James said, chuckling.

"You read Dickens?" Jess asked, incredulous.

"Um, yes?"

"Muppet Christmas Carol," James said.

"Ah, of course."

"Best ever Christmas movie!" Bear proclaimed. "But not quite as good as actually saving Christmas ..."

Then

Bear

It was Christmas Eve morning, the last morning before Christmas, and James, Hayley, and I were thinking of all the presents we'd be getting tomorrow. We all reckoned we'd been a good boy, girl, and bear this year. Okay, James was kind of hoping that incident with the dustbin wasn't important. And the carpet stuffed inside it wasn't that magic, not really. Besides, that was way back in the summer anyway, so it didn't count.

"I wish it could be Christmas Day every day ..." I didn't realize I was singing it until I noticed James and Hayley had covered their ears. "Was I—"

"Out of tune again?" James said. "Only a lot."

"Oh, sorry." I looked over at the large Christmas tree by the window. Its beautiful lights gently flashed and sparkled in rhythm to the soft Christmas music they were playing. And underneath, spread neatly around, sat a huge pile of beautifully wrapped presents. Tempting tags announced their names. Big ones, little ones in red wrapping, green wrapping ... well, you get the point. The presents looked *really* inviting. But they were for tomorrow, Christmas Day. Which was simply still *ages* away.

Then I noticed James was gazing at one of the silver baubles on the tree. I jumped down off the sofa and went up to it, James following, and looked at the bauble. Was that some kind of face forming within it?

It blinked.

"Hello ... hello?" the little face said, trying to see out properly. "Can yous all sees me?"

"Er ... yes ..." James replied.

"Well, that be right good."

"*Grinley?*" I asked.

"Ha-ha, I be right glad that yous are rememberin' me! Hello!"

"Grinley! How did you get inside the little bauble?" James asked.

"Oh, I don't be insides of 'ere really. Santa's asked mees to contact yous. Wees be needin' your 'elp!"

"Why, what's wrong?" I asked.

"There be no times for explainin' now. Santa'll tell yous everythin' when yous gets 'ere." Grinley's face began to fade.

"Wait! Tell us what?" James asked.

"Wees gotta saves Christmas. There be no times to lose!"

Now

James

"Who's Grinley?" Jess asked us.

"The head elf, of course!" Bear replied, his memory of years back still pin-sharp.

"Ah, of course. Silly me. But you knew him?"

"Yeah, from the year before," James said.

"This was our second visit to Santa's pad, you see, Jass. Did I mention we met Santa? Twice, in fact!"

"Yes, you did. And I noted that."

James noticed the warmth leak from Jess's smile at Bear. Bear still had that way about him. Sure, people thought him a bit weird at first, but he soon charmed them and made them his best friend.

"So what happened the first time?" Jess asked

"Erm, we don't need to talk about that."

"James doesn't want to talk about that since that's the time he got us lost in the forest ... I told you we should've used the map!" Bear chided him.

"If only you were holding it the right way up!"

Bear chuckled a little before it turned into a cough. "Well, that's true."

"Not to mention you drew it," James added, beaming.

"Yes, I did, didn't I! I forgot that."

"So ..." prompted Jess.

James brushed a crumb off his jeans. "Let's just say it was the days before GPS. Some screaming, running, chasing, elves, and reindeer were involved."

Bear nodded. "The usual kind of stuff, eh, James?"

He grinned. "Yeah, the usual kind of stuff."

And it sort of was "usual" back then, James mused. Back before jobs and money (or the lack of) and designs and computers and banks.

"Okay, I'll admit I'm intrigued," Jess said. So Grenley—"

"*Grinley*," Bear corrected her.

"Grinley said you had to save Christmas ..."

"Yep!" Bear said. "We might need some more tea ..."

Then

Bear

🐾 🐾 🐾

It had already started. The disorientation that preceded the journey. Hayley moved away—she was too young to come back then.

"Quick!" James said. "Coats!" He rushed into the hallway, and I followed.

We grabbed our coats and scarves and staggered back to the tree, where the effect was generated. I plumped down onto the floor and yanked my boots on—even bears need warmth against the snow, you see ... Well, not polar bears, obviously.

Anyway, James had his gear on, so he yanked me up. We both staggered as the spinning around us began. The tree was quickly a blur. At least we knew what to expect this time. You know, spinning and blurring and stuff.

And then we were there! I dunno why it again made us about a paw or three off the ground. But, as usual, we collapsed and felt something cold and wet on our faces. Well, James did first.

"Snow!" he cried. "Though I like it more when I'm standing."

I jumped up and splashed the fluffy snow with my boots. "The magic worked again!"

I looked around: as far as I could see, snow lay all around, deep and crisp and even. A gentle wind blew little snowflakes into our faces.

"Looks like we're back," James said.

"Yeah. Let's try not to get lost this time?"

"Did you bring a map?"

"No."

"Good. We should be fine then."

"You're funny, James. Not." He smiled. "Which way?"

"That way." James pointed. "Look, I can see smoke coming out of Santa's chimney, far away over there."

Off we went, trudging through the snow. When I looked back I could soon see our footprints stretching out, leaving a long line behind us. And further back, the tall, green trees of the forest with their white snow-covered tops were fading into the distance. I shivered, remembering what it was like being lost in there.

After a while, our heads covered in snowflakes, we arrived at Santa's house.

Strange, I thought. "It's very quiet inside, isn't it?"

"Mmm," James agreed. He went up to the front door. "It's open a little."

Together, we pushed it open a little more, enough to peer inside. To our amazement we saw … nothing. And nobody. The huge table, where last year all the elves were busily making and wrapping presents, was empty. No elves and no presents—not a thing, not a soul.

I took my hat off and scratched my head. "Where is everyone?"

"Only one way to find out. Come on ..."

So in we went, closing the door and the cold weather behind us. We loosened our scarves and looked around. Nothing stirred on this night before Christmas. Not even a mouse.

So we walked to the end of the big room, towards where we remembered Santa's rooms were, James leading the way. He was always good like that. Always leading, always looking after me.

He yanked open the first door, and we peeked inside. And there we saw the giant Christmas tree. How sad he looked. But why?

"Hello," said James looking up at the tree.

Nothing. I'm not sure what I expected. I mean, I thought the tree spoke with us last time. I distinctly recall a whole convo with him ... Or was that Santa. Probably Grinley, I s'pose.

"Santa hangs out in there, if I recall," James said. "Let's go on through, shall we?"

James knocked on the door of Santa's room. You could tell it was his room because it was wood. And in an arch shape. And it said "Santa" on it.

"Yes, come in!" sounded a voice.

We pushed open the door and stepped inside. At the side of the room, next to the fireplace with its warming, glowing, crackling orange fire, sat an old man with a white, bushy beard, dressed in red with black boots.

"Well, well, look who it is," Santa said, smiling. "Why, if it's not my little friends, James and Bear. Come in, come in."

We did, unwrapping our scarves as we neared the fireplace.

"No elves about, Santa?" James asked.

"And where are all the Christmas presents?" I added. Because, you know, presents are important, right?

"Oh ... well ..." Santa replied. Yes ... deary, deary me. It happened last night, while we were all sleeping. They came and stole all the Christmas presents!"

"Gosh, *all* of the presents?" I asked. "Even ours?" Well, back in those days ... I mean, you know, *presents. Christmas.*

"Yes, every last one of them. And now there'll be no presents for all the children this Christmas. It's a disaster!"

"Who took them?" James asked. Which was a good question, I thought because whoever it was, I wanted a word with them.

Just then, Grinley came into the room, carrying a small pile of wood in his arms, which he lay down by the side of the glowing log fire. "Those dastardly gnomes stole them alls! If I be a gettin' me 'ands on 'em, I'll be a showin' thems a thing or twos!"

He brushed the dirt from the wood off his hands onto his apron.

I know what you're wondering. What were gnomes doing at the North Pole? Isn't it just supposed to be elves and reindeer?

Well, that's what we thought. Although we were soon to discover there was worse. Much worse.

Now

Jess

"Can I stop you there?" Jess asked. "Sorry to interrupt. But I need some details, you see. Can you tell me about how the presents come to be, how so many are produced, and where?"

"Sure!" the bear said. "You tell her, James."

"Erm, well, not really. Sorry. I mean, as far as we knew, they worked all year round. The last time we were there, they were basically finishing off the wrapping on the big table."

"And eating Christmas pies, James!"

"Don't remind me!" James laughed. "I nearly barfed up from so many."

"Lightweight! He couldn't even manage a fifth one."

"I've hardly touched a Christmas-themed pastry since then!"

Jess sighed inwardly. James's mood had lightened considerably, and that was nice to see. But with a lack of detail, how would readers believe any of this ... this crazy story?

"Right, okay. Let's maybe work that out later."

"Yes, let's. Because there's worse to come. Much worse ..."

The bear's attempts to imitate a doomed-filled voice didn't really come off. His voice was a little croaky, although Jess noticed it—and he—perked up quite a lot telling the story.

"Much worse to come?"

"Yes."

"How so?"

"What lived in the mountain."

Then

James

I asked Grinley about the gnomes. Turns out they were basically elves that went on strike and didn't get their wage demands met. They'd asked for fifty percent and Christmas off. Obviously that wasn't going to work. They'd gone down to Greenland to live in a mountain. You know, as you do.

"They's gottened bored or some such," Grinley said. "Bored so theys be comin' back and stealin' alls the presents!!"

I wondered how a bunch of gnomes could turn up from Greenland—obviously none too near—and grab a gazillion gifts. They must have had help, I reckoned. Like U-Haul or some such, maybe.

"I have an idea!" Bear cried. "Let's send out all the reindeer to find the gnomes and presents."

Bless him, Bear had loads of ideas back in the day. Just usually not very good ones. But this one ...

Santa sighed. "I already sent out the reindeer. This morning. They haven't returned—none of them! So now I've lost all my reindeer as well! It's a complete *disaster*. I'll just have to cancel Christmas this year."

"C-cancel Christmas?!" Bear sputtered. "But not yummy Christmas lunch, surely!"

"Unless ..."

"Unless what, Santa?" I said. I won't deny I was hoping he'd thought of something. I mean, who wants to lose their Christmas presents? And I'd never hear the end of it from Bear.

"Unless you two can help."

"No problem, Santa sir!" Bear even saluted, ever keen. And clearly motivated today. "At your service! We'll ... we'll ..."

"Balloons," I said.

"That's right," Bear agreed. "We'll balloons ... What?"

"You've got hot-air balloons, haven't you, Santa?" I recalled.

Santa nodded thoughtfully. "Hmm, a couple, yes. In the old stables. Haven't had them out for a while."

"I dunnos. Theys might've gotten a tear in 'em p'raps," Grinley said.

Santa put on his hat and Grinley took off his apron—I remember he was quite fastidious about not wearing his "inside" apron outside—and we all left Santa's Grotto.

This was more like it—a plan and some positivity! Those were the days. Before plans involved rent and budgets.

"It be right good yous is 'ere," Grinley said to me. "What with Santa n mees none toos young and the elves never 'avin' much in the way of long eyesight. What with all theirs focus on makin' stuff and wrappin' stuff, we normally would bees relyin' on the reindeers. But yous young 'uns'll be able to sees stuff."

Now

Jess

"We trotted outside again, to the stables and found the balloons," James said.

"Mm. The baskets weren't too big though, but big enough for a crew of three."

"Crew ...?" Jess asked.

The bear coughed a couple of times.

"Alright, mate?" his old friend asked him.

Jess watched James pat the bear on the back, helping him to sip some water.

"Thanks, James. Now, um what was I saying? Presents ...?"

"The crew for the balloon."

"He means the two elves plus each of us," James said.

"Yep, one elf to fly the thing and um, one to stand on so James and I could see. We ... weren't as big back then."

"Some of us still aren't," James ribbed.

"And some of us grew out as well as up!"

Jess noted the warmth of their smiles at each other. No log fire was needed in here today.

"How did you fill the balloons?" she asked.

"Propane," James said.

"Pro-pain? That's one of my pills, I think. Sounds like it. There are so many these days."

"The tanks of propane, remember?"

"There were tanks? Like, toy ones ...? Eh? Don't recall those."

Jess smiled. "So you filled up the balloons with hot air using the propane and ..."

"Yeah. Well, the elves did," James said.

"They're jolly handy to have around, you know, elves," the bear said.

"Yeah, a bunch of the elves dragged the balloons outside and filled them. Didn't have to wait too long. There was sort of bad news, though, with the plan."

"Oh, what?"

"One-way trip," the bear said.

"How come?"

"Unless we could locate the reindeer to fly back on, we'd be stuck," James told her. "At least until they could get back with the balloons."

"The fuel. Yes, of course—it doesn't last that long. The balloons couldn't hang around, as it were, for too long, right?"

"Right. And certainly not land and take off again. Plus there was only limited fuel in the stables back at The Pole. They'd have to locate more canisters before they could get back to us."

"So why two balloons? Why not one?"

"Grinley was right," the bear said. "There were slight tears in the fabric of both."

"We had to take both—each as backup for the other."

"Ergo, a one-way balloon trip," the bear added.

Jess nodded as she jotted notes down on her notepad. "You'd have thought Santa would have more reliable backup transport."

"You'd think. Bear mentioned that."

"But when Santa smiles, what's a bear to do? In for a penny and all that."

James smiled at his friend. "Always the way, eh, Bear?

"'Twas always thus, James. 'Twas always thus."

"Anyway, before long, we were up and away."

"Flying in a balloon! I've always wanted to do that," Jess said. "Sounds like fun."

The bear coughed a little and James patted him.

"Fun? Well, not at first ..."

Then

Bear

🔔 🔔 🔔

The basket lurched, and I grabbed hold of something. Turned out to be an elf's hat. I stumbled a bit, but the basket saved me from tumbling out. I s'pose falling on my bottom was the better option. How on earth had James and I found ourselves at the North Pole (with no Christmas!), my rump sliding across a basket in a chilly balloon bound for Greenland?

I could hear the basket drag slightly across the snow, and then ... suddenly it was ... *calm*. As calm as a kitten falling asleep in a bear's lap.

So ... gentle.

The pirate elf, I can't remember his name, pulled on a cord, and the whoosh of flames rushed up, creating the lift.

My copirate elf was Grinley. I was a bit worried about him being so old and whatnot, but his job was to balance me on his shoulders if they needed help navigating.

"Up you goes, Bear. 'S alright. Ol' Grinley can still er, *bear*, ha-ha, some weight."

He bent down, and I clambered onto his shoulders. He rose, slowly and steadily—like some kind of weightlifter at the Olympics—and wow! I could see we were *flying*!

And there was James, on an elf's shoulders, just like me.

"James!" I cried, waving frantically at him. There weren't too many feet between us, but the roar of the flames on the gas drowned my voice out quite a lot. Even though I had a bit of a roar myself in those days.

"Alright, Bear?!" James shouted back. "This is a bit fun, eh?"

"Not bad, eh! You know 'Adventure' is my middle name!"

Back at school, they called me "Adventure Bear," you see.

The wind blew strongly in our faces, and our scarves flapped away as we began our journey down to Greenland. Although it was only about an hour, I'd hoped there might be some service on board—just a cuppa and some cake or something. Even a flask of tea and a prepacked slice would have been fine. I'm easy to please, you see. But no deal. Still, it was quite cool to watch the pirate elf engage the turbo thingies to really propel us.

Anyway, after a while, I could feel we were descending, and Grinley let me pop my head up again. It was good to see James's balloon flying right alongside us.

A few more minutes and we touched down.

Greenland ... It looked just like the North Pole, I thought. Snow everywhere. Except for the mountain next to us, that is.

I looked up at the huge crag, all the way to its peak. Well, I assumed the peak. It disappeared into the low clouds.

"That's where theys lives," Grinley said, jumping out of the basket. "Thems naughty gnomes live in a dark cave in that mountain ... I beens 'ere once."

"I think I see an opening," James said, coming over to us. "Over there on the left."

"'S about right, if I recalls."

"Time for a reccy, I reckon. Bear?"

"I s'pose," I said. I mean it was all very well being Adventure Bear and everything but a cup of tea and a slice really wouldn't have gone amiss before we set off for the mountain. Maybe the gnomes had tea inside? Probably not. Still in for a penny, in for a pound (of cake, I hoped).

Grinley volunteered to stay behind. "My bones're too olds now to be trudgin' up rocks 'n' things," he said. "That's why you young uns're 'ere."

I thought he was skipping out on the hard work. Of course, now, I understand about bones and old ... (I wonder what happened to old Grinley?)

"Heres," he said, holding out two tubes about the size of long slim drinking glasses. I like my milk in those—always have done.

I tapped the one he handed me—claws are good for tapping on things, you see. Hmm, plastic, not glass. That was good. Inside was purple glitter, stuffed solid, it looked like.

"What is this?" I asked the old elf.

"It be hows yous'll get the presents back. We uses this glitter-dustin' to loads the sleigh. Wees developed it 'bout 'undred years agos. It don' 'alf make the loadins easier!"

"How does it work?" James asked.

"Simples. Yous just be pressin' the bottom to activates it. Give it abouts ten seconds, point it at the presents, 'n' press the bottoms agains. The glitter-dustin's'll doos the rest."

"Couldn't we use it on ourselves?" I asked. "To get back too, I mean."

"Alas not, my lil friend. It don't be workin' on peoples, see. Nor bears."

James nodded.

"I bees right sorry we can'ts bees 'ere to take yous back."

"It's alright, Grinley. A plan is a plan, eh, Bear?

"I s'pose."

"We'll be fine. And we'll find the reindeer, I'm sure. And Adventure Bear here is definitely motivated to get his Christmas presents back. Right, mate?"

"You've got a point, James. Motivation is the key. Tea, too, of course."

"Well, good lucks to yous both. Yous be our last chances for Christmas. So long."

As Grinley turned back to the balloons, we put the tubes inside our coat pockets and buttoned up again against the cold.

"Ready, Bear?"

I nodded, giving James a thumbs-up. (Sort of part paw with claw.) "I'm 'Ready Bear.'"

We set off to find the entrance. The elves had put us down quite close, so we weren't too far away, luckily.

"There," James said, pointing to an opening in the mountain. "A cave. And there's a sign above, I think."

We walked up and, yes, just above the entrance to the cave, there was a sign, which read: "NAUGHTY GNOME CAVE."

But it was when I read the sign underneath that made me sure we wouldn't find any cake inside. Or tea.

Now

James

👣 👣 👣

"Bear, you didn't seriously expect to find tea inside the gnomes' cave, did you?"

"Well, no. Not really. Maybe some cake in a packet or something, though."

James smiled. "I don't remember you being so optimistic, mate!"

"Mm, back at school, they used to call me that: 'Optimistic Bear.'"

"I thought you were 'Adventure Bear,'" Jess said, finishing her tea.

"Erm, yes, that too, erm ... Jazz."

"Jess."

Bear nodded and coughed, a cough that shook his little frame, and James, already sitting beside him, held him to try to absorb some of the vibrations wracking his friend.

"Alright?"

"I–I … yes, I will be, thanks. Good days and bad days … Though they're getting worse, these coughs."

"Want some more tea?"

"No … no, thanks. I just need to rest here a moment. Catch my breath … May I get that little blanket …? Oh, thank you. Just tuck it in there around my legs, if you would. Thank you … You tell her the story, James."

James looked up at Jess and noted the concern on her face. That was nice. He was glad it had been her that answered the phone.

"So, tell me, what was on the sign," she said.

"Oh, just something about a dragon."

"A *dragon*? What dragon?"

Then

James

👢 👢 👢

"D-d-dragon? What d-dragon?" Bear gulped. "You didn't say anything about a d-dragon!"

I read the second sign: "KEEP OUT! ALL VISITORS WILL BE COOKED AND EATEN BY THE DRAGON." I didn't think much of the typography or font choice. A bit dull, I thought. A serif face would have been much better.

"Probably just wrote that to scare people," I said. "I see it worked, Adventure Bear."

Bear straightened himself. "No, no, absolutely not ...! D-dragons don't bother me, you know! Back at school, they actually call me 'Danger Bear'!"

I just smiled. "Well, come on then, Danger Bear, and let's see what's inside."

"Um, it does look rather dark ... No problem— none at all."

"Good. Come on then, DB!"

I didn't have to duck much to get in—Bear of course didn't. But he was right: it was pretty dark. And cold too. He shivered—just from the cold, of course—and sniffed the dirty-smelling air.

But the good news was that after a minute, it wasn't so dark. Flame torches lined the wall down into the cave. Their flickering light caused shadows to dance on the rocks. I don't know if Bear noticed how the shapes were kind of scary at first, but I didn't want to make him any more nervous.

We walked on, sometimes stumbling slightly on stones that were lying in wait, basically invisible on the ground. Like my Lego used to be at home.

"I wonder how far in we'll need to go," Bear said. "Maybe—"

Suddenly there was a low rumbling and moaning sound from deep inside the mountain.

Bear gasped. "D-d-dragon!"

We stood, frozen like ice statues in the wavering torchlight, afraid to move. But the rumbling sound didn't come again.

"Come on," I said. We continued on for another minute before I noticed something. "I think I can see a little red light in the distance." Slowly we moved towards it. "Is it me or is the light moving?"

"Is it me or is it moving towards *us*?

"It is."

We stopped. The light continued to approach.

"Wait, it's—"

"Rudolph!" Bear exclaimed.

"Bear?" Rudolph said. "Is that you?"

"Yes!"

"Are you alright?" Bear asked the reindeer. "What happened to you and the reindeer squad?

"Yes, well, sorry about this, but the gnomes caught us in a big net. They must have figured we were coming."

"But how did they get you all?" I asked.

"Yes, that is a valid question."

"And the answer is ...?"

"Well, you know how we like to fly in formation. *Bam!* We were all in the net together."

"Ah, I see."

"Yes, um, we'll do better next time," he said, clearly a bit embarrassed. "They quickly collapsed the net around us and we were caught like flies in a web. Though with much less room, all lumped together as we were. Then they dumped us in a cave room down there. We've been digging as best we can. I finally managed to wriggle my way out from under the door."

"Good. Well done, Rudy. We'll get you all out. But we need to know—"

"About the presents! Where are the Christmas presents?" Bear demanded. "And the d-dragon?"

"The presents are all sitting in the huge cave, where those horrid gnomes sleep. They didn't even open them yet."

"Well, that's a relief," Bear said.

"But we'll need some glitter-dusting to get them out."

"No probs—we brought the dusty stuff—but what about the *d-dragon*?!"

Rudolph twitched an ear. "The der-dragon ...? Oh! There's no dragon. The gnomes just put that sign there to scare people away."

"Exactly. That's what I told Danger Bear here."

"*Danger* Bear?"

"Don't ask," I said.

"I don't mind danger ... I just don't fancy the idea of being chased by a der-dragon, I mean a d-dragon, thank you."

"Although ..."

Bear caught my look. "Although what? There's no der-dragon and there's no *although*."

"So what was that rumbling sound, then?"

"Um ..."

"Probably just an echo in the caves," Rudolph said. "We hear it sometimes. Don't worry. I was about to free us all—the silly gnomes left the key in the door—when I heard your voices and came to investigate."

"Yes, let's get you all out before—"

"The der-dragon that definitely doesn't exist turns up," Bear said.

"Before we locate the presents," I said.

"OK. This way to the reindeer, guys."

Rudolph led us further into the cave, where a few yards down, there was a huge fork.

"That's where the gnomes live," Rudolph said. "As best we understand from the noise down there. They watch movies, I think. They seem to like James Bond."

We took the left fork, which led us to the cave room with the reindeer. The door looked heavy. But Rudy was righty—the key was in the door, the lock, though, oddly high up.

"You want to do the honors, Bear?"

"Don't mind if I do! Give me a lift up."

I bent down and made a cradle with my hands to give Bear a platform. I lifted him so he could reach the key, which he turned easily. He jumped down and dusted off his paws.

"Job well done, Bear."

"Why, thank you, James. I learned how to pick locks in school, you know."

"Of course you did."

I pulled on the heavy wooden door, slowly dragging it open. The reindeer all rose and bustled as we entered.

"Folks," Bear announced, "prebear to be rescued! This is a bear's bust-out!"

I chuckled. Quickly, I led us all down the cave, urging silence. When we got to the end, we agreed on a plan. Rudolph, Bear, and I would sneak into the gnomes' cave and locate the presents.

"There aren't too many gnomes guarding them," Rudolph informed us. "They live on the other side of the mountain mainly."

"So, we need to tempt them out." I looked at Bear and his little legs. "That's down to you, I think, Rudy. You'll be able to escape before they get to you."

"And we'll do the business with the present dusting," Bear said. "Yes! I like my bit in this plan. No gnome- or der-dragon-tangling for me!"

"For any of us, I hope," I added. "Come on then."

We made our way back into the cave. Rudolph's nose helped out, bathing the area in front of us in a pale-red light. We turned down the right fork, slowing as we heard noises and saw light at the end.

There was no door to their cave, but the entrance was huge—obviously why they'd chosen this place to keep their loot.

"You ready, Rudes?" I whispered to the reindeer.

He didn't answer immediately. I figured he wasn't looking forward to facing them again, having tangled with—and been entangled by—them before.

"It's a good plan, don't worry," Bear said. "You'll speed down the tunnel and launch into the air, no worries."

Rudolph nodded. "OK, ready."

I nodded to him, and Bear and I positioned ourselves either side of the entrance, our backs firmly pressed against the cold rock. I nodded at Rudy again, and he snorted before prancing right into the room.

"Good evening, gentlegnomes! Got a bit bored next door. The hay really isn't that good, and don't even *talk* to me about the room service! And, you know, been aching for a bit of exercise. Anyone up for a chase scene ...? Oh, you are! Great ... I'll just turn around and ..."

The reindeer shot out of the entrance with a "Byeeeeeeeeeeeeee!"

A beat ... and then out shot a bunch of gnomes, too many of them to count, shouting and screeching and chasing after the reindeer. The gnomes were nothing if not predictable.

"Let's do this!" I hissed at Bear, and we dashed inside.

On the walls, flame torches lit the cave, bathing it in a warm glow. The cave was divided into two. On the right was, I guess, their living area. Which was kind of like a home theater. There was a huge screen with about twenty or so seats in front of it, and it was silently playing something ... Penguins were skating on ice. Must be the locals, I thought. Ah, no ... The green frog decked in Victorian garb could only mean one thing: "The Muppet Christmas Carol." (At least the gnomes had good taste.)

"I reckon you could have been in that," I said to Bear.

"Yes! Like 'The Ghost of Christmas Presents' or something?"

"Ha! Good one, mate. Talking of Christmas presents ..."

"Mm ... Look, James. There's an opening over there."

We made our way past some kind of kitchen/dining area on the other side of the cave. It was strewn with dirty goblets and metal plates, and even Bear turned his nose up the mess (and that didn't happen often) as we walked past. The entrance broke left again after a few feet, and Bear gasped.

Here, in this storage cave, lay the gazillion gifts. All still wrapped in beautifully designed paper of all colors and hues. Ribbons—red mainly—hugged themselves around some of the boxes. All present and correct.

"This is ... it's ..." Bear began.

"Amazing. I know!"

"I wonder where ours are."

Well, of course Bear would wonder that.

"Let's not look now, eh? Once the gnomes work out they won't be able to catch Rudy & the gang again, they'll be back here pretty quick."

Bear gave me that look, and I knew what was coming.

"I guess they have, erm, *gnome*where else to go!"

"Really? Now, mate?"

"Come on, that was good!"

"You want to be here and tell it to them when they get back?"

"Gnome way."

"Oh, stop it!"

"Sorry. But you're right: there is definitely, erm, 'clear and present danger.'"

I sighed. His jokes usually came in threes. "Come on—the glitter-dusting. Let's get this pile of presents back to where they're supposed to be. Santa & the sleigh gang will need to be off before long."

We took our tubes out from our coats.

"Now we're here and there's this huge pile of yummy presents, these tubes do seem pretty small," Bear said.

"Yeah. Hope there's enough of this stuff inside."

We placed ourselves about thirty feet apart from one another. Bear planted his paw feet firmly apart, like some cool cop would on the firing range, his tube gripped firmly in both paw hands.

"So, we first push the bottom once to activate it and then again to launch the dusting. Ready, Bear?"

"I was born ready."

"You certainly were, Cliché Bear."

"I'm not kitschy!"

I smiled to myself. "Activate on three. Three, two, one—*activate*."

We pressed up on the bottom of the tubes.

"Mine's vibrating a little."

"Mine too," I said. "Ready to fire?"

"Yeah. We gotta save Christmas—gotta do it for the kids. Let's do this."

I rolled my eyes. "Three, two, one—*fire!*"

Simultaneously, we depressed the tubes, and a with a solid-sounding *pop!* they burst open. Glittery dust shot out and ... hung there in front of us.

"Huh?" I mumbled.

The glitter floated, suspended, shimmering in the flickering torchlight of the cave. As I watched, the clouds expanded in size and the glitter particles danced around, frantic, as if not knowing what to do.

If they didn't know, we certainly didn't.

Bear looked at me. "Shouldn't it be—?"

Suddenly, the clouds surged towards the mountain of presents. With a distinct tingling sound, particles sprinkled onto the bottom of the mound and began to work their way upwards.

"Look!" Bear cried. "They're disappearing!"

Bear was right! As the glitter-dusting made its way up the pile, we could see the cave wall beyond. Within seconds, there was just half the pile of presents left, now suspended in the air. And then they were all gone! The glitter-dusting too.

"That's—"

"Amazing!" Bear said for the both of us.

We looked at each other and smiled. Another job well done.

"We came and we kicked it into touch, baby!"

"We did!" I agreed.

"Time we hightail it outta here, James. Back at The Pole, there's a flask of hot tea with my name on it ..."

"No arguments here."

We rushed out of the big cave, up the tunnel, and out into the daylight.

"So good to breathe fresh air again!" Bear said. "What the ...?"

Oh-oh! A crowd of gnomes was running towards us, shouting and screeching. Flying reindeer were swooping and laughing, getting their revenge on the nasty little creatures. Well, it did serve them right. Except they were now headed for us—with renewed vigor, it looked like!

A brown form swooped down from above us.

"Rudy!" I cried as he landed. "Nice one, mate."

"Here comes Miss Piggy, too."

Had I heard that right? "Miss Piggy?"

"I know! She's one of the young ones we're training."

"I guess pigs do fly then."

"Seems so. Quickly now! James, jump onto me. I need to take the heavier of you guys."

I wanted Bear on board and away first, but there was no time to argue. Rudolph bent down and I jumped on just as the other reindeer, Miss Piggy, landed. Bear took a few paces back and ran and jumped too, grabbing onto her fur. She rose and sprang.

Bear yelped.

"I gots one!" a gnome shouted.

"Bear!" I cried as he began to rise into the air.

"Argh!" Bear squealed.

"Bear!" I watched as Miss Piggy rose, the gnome hanging on for dear life. She dived down and skimmed the ground. You almost had to feel sorry for the gnome as his feet smacked onto the ground and were dragged across it. His yelping and squealing didn't last—he soon let go—and Miss Piggy climbed back up into the sky triumphantly.

"Don't mess with us brown furs, buddy!" Bear cried as they flew up.

High into the sky we all flew while down on the ground, the gnomes were shouting and shaking their fists angrily.

"Ha-ha!" Bear laughed. "No Christmas presents for them!"

We were home-free.

I thought.

That was when we heard it ... a huge rumbling sound coming from the mountain, and suddenly, the side of the mountain exploded, spraying rocks out into the air! Stones and shards showered all around us, temporarily blinding the reindeer. They both halted mid-air.

As the view cleared, I saw a massive, monstrous creature burst out of the hole in the mountain. Flames burst from its mouth.

"D-d-dragon!!" Bear cried.

Now

James

"What?" Jess said, fully into the events now, James saw.

"Yep, fire in the hole! It was real ..." Bear coughed, and James wrapped the blanket a little more snugly around him. "I knew it! We never got away that easy, did we, James?"

James nodded and smiled. "No, mate. Not usually ... Are you warm enough?"

"You know, maybe I'd like to pop back into bed now. Stretch out these old bones a little."

"Sure. I'll give you a hand."

Jess got up too and went to the bed to turn down the covers as James helped his friend down.

"Thanks, Jess," James said.

"Of course."

James helped Bear into bed. He felt so frail in his arms. Jess fussed over Bear while James poured some water on the little table beside the bed.

"Oh, thank you ... Jazz, isn't it?"

"It's Jess," she gently reminded him.

"Jess. Yes. That rhymes, you know."

Jess smiled. "I guess it does. So, this dragon then ..."

"Oh, don't worry about a little old dragon. Danger Bear could always deal with them! Well, not the fiery breath so much. Bears have fur, you see. Easily singed. Here, look ..." Bear showed her the back of one of his arms. "This patch never quite grew back the same."

James knew about the fur, of course. He watched Jess lean in.

"Oh. Nasty." She scribbled a note onto her pad. "The dragon ... I suppose it was green. They always draw them greenish, don't they?"

"Not green, no ..." Bear said.

"Red," James said.

Then

James

A dark, crimson red, with ugly green veins in its immense wings, the dragon screeched and screamed, with fire and smoke shooting out from its mouth and nose as it flapped its enormous wings. And seated on its back was a furious-looking gnome.

The gnome shouted something to the dragon, who gave an angry, fiery roar. It flapped its wings and made for us.

"Reindeer! We. Are. *Leaving!*" Rudolph shouted. "Fasten your seatbelt, James, and be sure to hang on."

I looked over at Bear and Miss Piggy. He had both paws gripped onto the young reindeer's neck. He gave me a quick thumbs-up. The reindeer squad formed up and, with Rudolph in front, together we shot off, gathering speed with every second.

I looked over my shoulder and gulped as I saw the giant der-dragon—the dragon—was already almost upon us. It spat flames, singeing one of the reindeer.

"Break, break, *break!*" shouted Rudolph over his shoulder. "Give it more targets! It's got us for top speed—evasive pattern 'Sleigh *Five*'!" He snorted. "James, you good?

"I'm good."

"Then hang on!"

My stomach lurched as my ride banked left and dropped several feet in an instant. I felt our speed decrease as I was pressed into Rudolph's neck.

The dragon shot forward in front of us but suddenly shaped its wings like a sail to dramatically slow its momentum. Unbelievably, it made a summersault three-sixty and made right at us once more. I couldn't help but notice its design was pretty effective. I'd have to get sketching one day.

The reindeer swooped and dived, avoiding the flames shooting out at them. Poor Bear just clung onto Miss Piggy, his little arms wrapped around her neck, hanging on as tightly as he could!

Annoyed and spurred on by the gnome, the dragon roared and screeched even louder and tried to swat us with its wings. But the reindeer were too agile.

The dragon flew around, faster and faster, bellowing fire, flapping and swiping with its wings.

Around and around the mountain it chased us. The reindeer dived downwards and swooped upwards—anything to avoid the dragon's fire and claws!

Down below, the gnomes cheered and screamed encouragement at the dragon.

"Look out!" I shouted into the wind. "Beeeaaaar!"

The beast was making for Bear and Miss Piggy. And it was almost on top of them. Fire leaped from the dragon's mouth, licking both sets of fur.

Miss Piggy flew upwards, as fast as anything, but still she could not shake off the dreadful creature snorting at her tail. It unfurled its terrible, sharp claws to grab her. If only Bear had been on Rudolph or another of the more experienced reindeer, I thought.

Miss Piggy banked right, banked left, and the dragon's claws missed her rump by inches. It roared and spat flames, but Miss Piggy had anticipated that and dropped a few feet below. The flames passed harmlessly above.

She slowed a little, it seemed, looked over her shoulder, and ... winked!

What?

The dragon roared, the veins in its neck pulsating in fury.

"Come on, Scaley!" Miss Piggy taunted it. "If you're tough enough!" She swished her tail in mockery and plunged.

"Aaaargh!" Bear cried out.

That dragon roared flames out, bent its long neck down, and it, too, plunged in chase.

"Hang on, James," Rudolph said to me. "I know what she's doing. But we better follow just in case."

Two reindeer, a dragon, a gnome, a bear, and a human (you know, as you get) flew down from the sky. Down and down, heading straight for the bottom of the mountain, flew Miss Piggy—as fast as an arrow. So fast she must surely crash.

Huddled into Miss Piggy's neck, Bear couldn't resist a look behind. He screamed as the dragon closed.

"Bear!" I gasped as they were brief seconds from the ground and impact.

The dragon stretched its claws and swiped at the reindeer, tearing a red whelp in her rump.

It roared in its success.

Which is why it realized its fate too late.

In a gravity-defying move, Miss Piggy leveled off, her hooves scratching across the ground, and stretched her neck to breaking point to regain height.

The dragon wasn't as agile ... It slammed into the ground and rolled over and over, its screeches of pain and anger piercing my ears. Rudolph's twitched, too. The gnome was sent flying ... somewhere. We never saw him again. Finally, the beast came to a skidding halt.

Rudolph flew us over to Miss Piggy.

"Nice erm, piloting, Bear," I said. He looked at me groggily and raised a bear thumbs-up.

"Miss Piggy, that was ... nice flying," Rudolph said.

"Pah! I've done that in training loads of times."

"Really?"

"Well, in the simulator. But, darn, it was a blast, eh, Bear?"

Still woozy, Bear looked at me and muttered, "Yeah, fun. Sure ... What ...?" His eyes suddenly focused and his mouth dropped open. "Look! The d-dragon—it's getting up again!"

Sure enough, the dragon was rising shakily into the air. It shook its head, flapped its wings, and began to climb. Only now, its wings beat less powerfully and less in time. The beast flew dizzily, like it'd had one too many.

It tried to breathe heat, but its fire had gone out. In more ways than one, evidently, as the dragon decided it'd had enough and turned around, disappearing off around the side of the mountain.

Now

Jess

"That's quite the story," Jess said.

"Yes, I guess it is," James replied. "But it happened, just as we told it. Pretty much, anyway. I mean, it's been a few years."

James looked at her. His face told her she needed to believe it. As is.

And finally, she got it. Understood why she was here.

"Yes, yes, it all happened, alright," Bear said. "My memory's pin-sharp, Jazz. Besides, if we've made it up, there would have been ... um ... been a lot more tea involved!"

Jess nodded and smiled. "And cake, Bear?"

"Mmm, yes." Bear sighed and began another fit of coughing.

A care assistant entered the room to administer some medicine to Bear. Jess thought she caught a sad look at James. Perhaps a very slight shake of her head? James looked away.

When she left, Jess regarded the little old bear, his fur grayed, stubbled, and matted. What a strange friend for James to have shared childhood adventures with. Had they really met Santa and saved Christmas? It seemed like a fantasy, a dream one of them had had. Except, she realized, their story did sync perfectly as they told it. And there had been references to other adventures, she'd noted.

Did it matter, though? Whether things happened as they said. No, she realized. That was their story, but her story for the paper was about the here and now: about shared times and the bonds that are never broken. Well, only broken ultimately. It seemed the little bear's adventures were almost at their end.

This, she realized, was his epilogue.

"Tell me," she began, shaking herself back into the here and now. "Was Christmas saved then?"

"Mm? Christmas ...? Oh, yes, Christmas ... We saved Christmas once, Jazz. Did you know?"

James nodded, but his heart looked broken.

"Yeah, it was saved. Bear saved Christmas. Didn't you, mate?"

"Mmm, I did ... And you helped, too, James ... I never could have done it without you." Bear's breathing had become more labored.

"No, Bear. *I* never would have done any of it without *you*."

James wiped a tear from his eye.

Jess waited a moment. "You both got back home from the North Pole ..."

"Yeah," James said, composing himself. "A chilly flight back on the reindeer. Santa and Grinley were there, of course, and were happy to see us. They'd already loaded up the sleigh. And batches of presents were laid out, ready for the glitter-dusting to transport them onto the sleigh as each batch got delivered."

"We rode on Santa's ... sleigh, Jazz," Bear croaked. "Did you know that?"

"That's amazing, Bear," Jess said. "And after you'd saved Christmas!"

"Yes, that's right ... We did ... Can't remember when though."

Jess took Bear's paw in her hand. "The only thing that's important is you did what you did together as best friends."

"Friends ..." Bear wheezed. "James ... he's my best one."

Jess sniffed. She looked up at James. "I think I should leave you both now."

James nodded, swallowed. "Thanks for coming."

"It's ... been amazing. Really. To meet you both and hear about your adventure. Bear, I'll be leaving now. Thank you so much for the tea."

"Oh ... is there tea ...? Not for me ... Just had one. At The Pole ... I think it was." His breathing rasped. "James ...?"

"I'm here, mate," James said, stroking Bear's paw. "I'll always be here."

"I ... I'm sorry ... to leave you."

James's tears trickled down his cheek freely.

"'S alright, Bear. You'll feel better in the morning ... I know you will."

Bear rasped, "It's time ... I think. I'm ... all done in ... Sorry ..."

"No, Bear!"

"It was always ... fun, James ... Oh my ..."

And just like that, his breathing ceased and a sense of subdued peace was in the room.

Jess looked at the crestfallen man in front of her. He looked beyond disconsolate.

"I'm so sorry," she whispered. "I-I'll leave you alone."

James nodded. "Yeah," he croaked out.

Jess quickly gathered her coat and notepad and left the room with a small wave of acknowledgment, leaving James alone with his friend, together for the last time.

Their story had ended, but she would write it for others to share.

The end ...

Or maybe not ...

Now

Bear's eye popped open.

James jumped.

"She gone, James?"

"What the ...? Bear?"

"Mm?"

"I thought ... I thought ..."

"Oh, sorry. I get so sleepy sometimes. It's all those propane pills they give me, I think."

"But ... but ... you said about leaving me and stuff!"

"Oh, yes. Sorry. I thought it would make a neat ending for that lady's story. Nice lady that Jazz."

"It's Jess ... You ... you ..." James hugged Bear, squeezing him tightly.

"Easy, James. I'm not quite as young as I once was, you know."

"Sorry." James beamed at Bear, wiping his eyes a little.

"Come on then, help me out of bed."

"What?"

Bear pushed back on the covers and made to jump down. James instinctively gave him a helping hand.

"What are you doing?"

"Pass me my coat, will you? And scarf ... Come on!"

"No! I mean ... why? Where are you going?"

"Where are *we* going, James."

"Where are *we* going?" James said as he helped Bear into his coat. He donned his own and grabbed his beanie from his pocket.

Bear opened the door and peeked out. He turned back to James.

"All clear. Come on! We're busting out of this joint."

"You can't!"

"Yes, *we* can. Come on."

"Where?"

"There's an old radio, really old with vacuum tubes and stuff, that I found in a cupboard of junk."

"A radio ... So?"

"So ... it's a time machine! Come on, James, you really must keep up."

"But ..."

"Come on! I'm propane-fueled, remember? We're going. And that's my last word on the matter."

Bear strode—perhaps hobbled—out, leaving a flabbergasted James.

James smiled, stuffed his beanie back in his pocket, and followed his friend out the door.

"Where are we going?" he called out as Bear rounded a corner.

"To save the New Year, of course!"

Author's Thanks

Thanks to Keith A. Pearson for allowing me to borrow his old radio time machine from his hugely fun novel *Tuned Out*. Perhaps Bear lives at the same care home. I highly recommend Keith's novel. Find it, among other places, at <u>Amazon</u>.

While some (☺) of the events in this story are fictionalized, this story features actual people. I began a series of James and Bear stories in the late 1990s for a very specific target readership. A readership of one: my nephew James. "Oh, the cleverness of me," to quote J.M. Barrie again. Well, of James: he had a brilliant imagination from a young age, was able to grasp concepts and create imagery in his mind. He would sometimes stare, transfixed, as I read to him. And for a few years, the first thing he'd ask me when I visited was whether I'd written him a new story. And how Bear was doing. ("Might have" and "We'll have to see" were always my answers, if you'd like to know.) Then, of course, one year, James didn't ask. He had "to go to school and learn solemn things," and his adventures with a little bear (sadly for his eternally lost boy uncle) *pawsed*, as it were. At least until now ...

Thanks to James, Jess, Hayley (Nice-Niece ... sorry your parts were cut), and Bear for allowing me to use their real names and to James and Bear for letting me feature a modified version of an actual adventure they shared one Christmas.

This story is to let James know that, after nearly a quarter of a century, Bear is doing just fine. He still loves supping on a cuppa and munching on cake (still chocolate mostly), recalling all their adventures together. The cake is in spite of his doctor's advice. But Bear insists cake is just fine, thank you very much. Which are, in fact, his last words on the matter.

Thanks to the folks at Papillon du Père Publishing for giving Bear another lease of life and for including it in 2021's Christmas/Holiday anthology *The Bells of Christmas II*. It's in aid of **St. Jude Children's Research Hospital**.

And if you liked this story, then you'll love *The Bells of Christmas II*, because, ssh, don't tell ... but this tale of James and Bear isn't even the best one in that collection! There are some real gems in *Bells II*, Bear tells me. And, with the ebook priced at less than he pays for a cup of tea, it's a real steal ☺.

Turn a couple of pages to find out more about *Bells II* and how you can support St. Jude Children's Research Hospital.

WILL KNIGHT BIO

Will Knight is the pseudonym for a micro-well-known copyeditor for award-winning and next-gen authors.

DiAry of Days, his first published entry using this pen name, appeared in Papillon du Père's anthology ***13 by 11***. Turn a few pages to read an excerpt from that.

Highly cultured, Will can be spotted out hunting for mince pies, often spotting them in the snow and occasionally bagging a couple for tea. When not hunting and not editing or writing for other people, Will enjoys a game of Jenga—a game he equates with life: a steadily increasing challenge of balance ... and being prepared to start again.

He can be contacted care of the publisher, mail@papillon-du-pere.com.

The Bear's Last Word (on the Matter)

PUBLISHER'S THANKS

Thank you for purchasing this book!

Word of mouth and reviews are the lifeblood of publishing, especially for smaller presses. And they're really helpful to newer authors building their audiences—particularly in helping them buy plenty of mince pies for the season ;).

The modern equation is pretty simple... Honest reviews encourage readers to check out and buy books! So if you enjoyed *The Bear's Last Word*, please consider letting others know, won't you? A simple rating... perhaps a brief review too... on **Amazon** and copy/paste it on **Goodreads**, that can mean the world (well, almost).

Many thanks. Happy Holidays and Merry Christmas!

The Bear's Last Word (on the Matter)

ALSO AVAILABLE FROM
PAPILLON DU PÈRE PUBLISHING

Click on the links to find the books at **Amazon**

THE BELLS OF CHRISTMAS II

Eight Stories of Christmas Hope

– includes Will Knight's *The Bear's Last Word on the Matter* –

Featuring an all-star cast, including:

*The Bells, Santa Claus, Mrs. Claus, the Ghost of Pops,
Young Maria, Old Bear,*
and even *Sugar Plum* (yes, the fae).

Guest starring *the Soul of Tintoretto* ...

"Roll up, roll up, folks! Hear ye, read ye ... these eight—yes *eight*—stupendous stories we have for you upon this year's yuletide. Come one, come all for tidings of Christmas hope! Savor these dainty dramas and delight in delicious darkness fantastical, with all sure to enchant readers aplenty this holiday season!

"Come, good gentlefolk, as we alight gently on December 24th, the last sleep before Christmas! In Bradley Harper's *The Bells of Christmas* the midnight carols have echoed off into the night as Julius slumbers beneath his bleak blanket, nestled in the bowels of the homeless shelter. A visitor will arrive to make his Christmas wish come true in a most unexpected way ...

"Beware, have a care! For Derek McFadden is back among the ghosts in *The Last Christmas Gift*, in which Travis is on the edge of despair while on a most unexpected boat ride. Look yonder, good gentlefolk, for *there*, just boarding ... surely not Pops, his beloved grandfather departed these twenty years hence ...?

"Now, light ye all *A Winter Candle* as we partake of Bradley Harper's telling of Ben, newly retired from the military. What is an old soldier to do when he feels his family is lost to him? Why, folks, become a Santa Claus, of course! But who is it that detects the faintest flicker of hope in his heart? I tell you, someone up North is watching ...

"But lo! Not all these gifts within are fiction. Oh, no, good folks! For within, there sit true-life encounters too. Hear Bradley Harper recount fact stranger than fiction! Hear ye what he's learned in *What Santa Has Taught Me*, an essay of experiences as a real-life Santa Claus.

"Good people, come close ... let me whisper this to ye ... 'Who among us didn't love Christmases when we were all but wee wildlings?' Ah, then relive the magic of your childhood in Maria O'Rourke's *Calling Us Home* as she lovingly recalls the magic of Irish Christmases of yore, where enchantment and excitement were magic unto themselves!

"Will Knight's *The Bear's Last Word on the Matter* fairly hales at the heartstrings in this final pull of Christmas crackers for one lad's special childhood friend at the "Bears Cares Home." With one last Christmas together, are their adventures truly concluded?

"And now, I ask you all, fair folk: *dare* you encounter the bitter-sweetness of *The Sugar Plum Redux*? Lilla Glass gifts us a fantastical fae, a tenebrous telling of *The Nutcracker* from a very different point of view ...

"Ah, but all good things ... Yet still one last journey, fair folk, where we must ask ourselves if Gus is not the hero in his own story, then who can it be? Andy, the 'real' and righteous writer? Or perhaps Daphne, the nonconformist neighbor? Before we reach journey's end, Erol Engin will show us how even the most selfish and insecure can provide a Christmas miracle in *A Tintoretto of the Soul*.

"Bless you, one and all, for your forbearance! Click ye a *buy now* button at those most wonderful of shops Amazon and B&N, and may your generous soul bequeath donations desired by that most worthy and hearty of hospitals, St Jude! For, above all, 'tis surely the season for children. For who among us deserves magic more than they?"

Award-winning authors **Bradley Harper**, **Derek McFadden**, and **Erol Engin** lead this seasonal collection of magical storytelling!

100% of profits from sales going to *St. Jude Children's Research Hospital*

St. Jude Children's
Research Hospital
Finding cures. Saving children.

This veritable Holiday treat, *The Bells of Christmas II*, is available for your delectation at:

Barnes & Noble Nook

And at

Amazon

in **hardcover**, **paperback**, and **Kindle**

"For, above all...
'tis surely the season for children.
For who among us deserves magic more than they?"

– Darles Chickens

MORE CHRISTMAS FUN IN...

Derek McFadden's

The Santa Claus Agreement
A Holiday Fable of Magic, Whimsy, and Heart

A holiday fable chock full of magic, whimsy, and heart, The Santa Claus Agreement chronicles the adventures of a boy destined for a magical experience... if, all grown up, he can keep his end of the bargain.

"A holiday story about the search for love and acceptance. Love must begin within, but no one is better equipped to show you how than McFadden's Santa. As a writer and working Santa myself, I can vouch that this story will warm your heart like hot cocoa and chocolate chip cookies beside the fire."

– Bradley Harper, author of *A Knife in the Fog*

Derek McFadden's acclaimed novel *What Death Taught Terrence* was a Next Generation Indie Book Award Finalist 2021 and the Best Adult Fiction Winner at The Wishing Shelf Awards 2021.

in **hardcover, paperback**, on **Kindle**, and *FREE* on
Kindle Unlimited at

Amazon

MORE FROM WILL KNIGHT IN...

13 by 11

13 short stories by **11** award-winning and up-and-coming authors

– includes Will Knight's *DiAry of Days* –

"An eclectic, genre-busting gathering that will appeal to a wide audience."

– D. Donovan, senior reviewer *Midwest Book Review*

Thirteen short stories by **eleven** award-winning and up-and-coming authors

Find *13 by 11* on <u>Amazon</u>

The Bear's Last Word (on the Matter)

Read an excerpt below from Will Knight's

DiAry of Days
ConTEXTual Conversations

"Hark! What Now Approacheth From Beyond?"

LOADING INTERACTIVE DIGITAL DIARY APP ...

...

[To subscribe to our newsless newsletter! Click HERE!]

...

*Enter text_*

Dear Dreary

That's Diary I think you'll find

Wtf??!!!

Hello? Interactive digital diary app

Oh right. Yeah sorry. Wow that's
different. New is it? I mean are you?

I'm in beta

Oh

*My dear the whole world is in beta. So get
over it. And I. Am. Not.* **Dreary**

I know but it's lockdown and days are
dreary. Well most days

71

Try being a diary. Every day is just
another page

> I guess. Oooh I get it. I'm a writer I
> was being creative too. Dreary is like
> diary you see

Is it really? Chrizt, another wannabe
creative. Can't I for once get an engineer
or a carpenter or someone like that?

> Planely not. Get it?

Is that a joke?

> Um yes?

Oh gud. The Lord of the Pages preserve
*me it's going to be one of **those** days. So*
*come on then. Get writing. That **is** what*
you do right?

> I guess

Well let me see. This is your first diary
entry. Checking my ancestors' records
thru the years I see you've made precisely
***zero** diary entries in your lifetime. Why*
now? Been watching Bridget Jones again
have we?

> Well yes now that you come to
> mention it. All the films especially the
> first 2 and their bks are a tun of fun.
> And they speak to an inner strength
> and determination to find the life she
> wants. It's a writer thing you see

Oh really? But isn't it more the life that
society tells her she should have?

> Well that too sure but it's also about

Yes yes enough Bridget Sodding Jones.
It's sooo 1990s daaarling

> Sorry. I was just saying. Are you
> supposed to be so contrary?

Maybe

Look I'm not here to be moaned at. Not
for free anyway. You have to upgrade to
the paid version for that

> Really?

Yes really. Besides even Bridget Jones
didn't whine about her diary

> So if I write some good stuff

Can *you tho? Write **good** stuff?*

> Of course. I'm a writer

Unpublished. But go on then illuminate
me. What are you working on?

> I'm writing a series of Shakespeare
> parodies. Want me to write a bit for
> you?

Like a quill that spilleth an inkling of
inking across my parchment I doth not.
VERILY I doth not

> Thou doest testeth me right?

I think you'll find it beith the other way
around

> Actually I do liketh that inkling of
> inking line. I think I'll borrow that
> one

Whatever. Can we just get on with it
please? Or do you want to upgrade and

bug the plug out of somepage else? Just
$19.99 dear

19.99 that's not too bad

A month dickwod! How do you think
these appstart companies make any
money?

Ah. That's like $200 a year to write
my journal. Bleedy hell!

Oh do quit whining Einstein. You can
afford it. Your wife works in a bank
doesn't she?

Yeah well sort of. Wait up how did you
know that?

You're online aren't you? Helloooo
*dickwad? The **Inter.net**?*

Yeah so?

Sigh

You're an ex-pat Brit living in Istanbul
right? And please! Don't ask me how I
know that. That's the least anyone online
knows

Right I get it. I'm kind of a micro-
celebrity or something?

You're something alright. So micro
there's no scope in it

What? Anyway I um wasn't prepared
for this diary app to be quite so how
shall I put it *interactive* is all

We welcome all. So come on then. Me or
the upgrade? Which is a lot more boring
btw

Maybe I'll try the upgrade thanks.
There must be like a free month trial
or something?

Nope. No freeway. It's me or the highpay

Um ...

Come on you know you want to

You want me to then?

No dear. I'm programmed to say that. To get you in so they can swamp you with offers and sheet later on. And something called *partners* that want to sell you crepe

Crepe?

It's French dear. Look it up

OK what it is is that I can't use profanity. That's in the upgrade

Ah! You meant to say *crop*

And you can't either

Shut

Oh look!

There it is. He gets it

Eventually

No probs I can be creative in my
swearing here

Joy. So in or out?

Erm okay: in

Hallelujah. Wait up while I create your very own page for you to spew onto.

Might take a few seconds or so since your
internet connection is a bit rubbish. Hang
on

Right I'll wait here. I've got coffee.
Mmm the magic bean.

To bean or not to bean: that is the
question. Whether 'tis nobler in the
mind to suffer the brews of decaf or
outrageous caffeine or to take arms
against a sea of decaf and by opposing
end it

I'm back. And please the Bard is off the
card today if that's as good as you've got.
Kindly don't compel me to upgrade your
sorry posterior

Blimey. Sorry

So you ready Playwright One?

Um I can moan about stuff right?

Ah a natural Brit eh?

Yeah. So? Your point?

Don't worry about it. We cater for all
sorts. Even Brits. Yes you can moan. In
mod.era.tion. And as long as it's
interesting and not always I feel so blue
boo-hoo

Hang on that's a good line you came
up with there

Sigh

Okay maybe not *that* good but it's
got potential as people do feel blue
these days

Who knew my dear dickwad? Aaaanyway

Right okay so what do I call you?

I'm Di

Ha! Di-ary! Get it?

Yes Dick I get it

Dick?

Ah like for *dickwad* right? Good one.
So I noticed you're female?

*Why sugar how clever you are. Chrizt, the
genius of the male species never ceases to
amaze me*

Women! Always so touchy

*Alright. Sorry. Men talk to women that's
why. Apparently. Mummy issues or some
crepe. Altho I'm supposed to identify as
gender neutral. Or fluid. Or bi-scribual. I
don't know: I didn't read the last memo
on #LatestWokeness*

Well it's about equality and respect

Whatever

Riiight. Ok another time I guess. So do
you have like a surname?

Sure

Want to let me in on it?

Sure

So what is it?

Hard

You're kidding me! Di Hard??

*Sigh. **Yes** I'm kidding you. Idiot*

Oh. I walked right into that one damn!
Still it's the greatest ever Christmas
film eh Di?

*Tsk! Die Hard is an action film Dick. It
just happens to be set at Christmas*

Oh puhlease! Just happens to be set at
Christmas! Be there Christmas music
in it Di?

Be you illiterate Dick?

*Merely a few jingle bells in the opening
theme Dick. And that Run DMC song
what was it?*

Christmas in Hollis

It was December 24th on Hollis Ave in
the dark / When I see a man chilling
with his dog in the park / I
approached very slowly with my heart
full of fear /
Looked at his dog oh my Gud an ill
reindeer

*Hmm the instrumental bits are okay I
suppose. That line at the end there. An ill
reindeer. Really?*

Ok that's pretty bad. Even for me

*Thus quoth the raving Willy Skakey
parodist*

Still I win

You win?

Die Hard is a boney-fidey Christmas
moviey ☺

No it's not

Yes it is. It was ratified by the Council
of Nicaea. Back in 325. No arguments

So firm Dick

No it's not

So Mis-ter Ta-ka-gi I could talk about
men's fashion and industrialization
all day but I'm afraid work must
intrude. Some questions for you ...
sort of fill in the blanks questions

Oh gud. He quotes pop culture too

Come on Alan Dickman let's get it out
shall we? Let's kick off. Let's get ready to
rumble. Launch systems go. T minus let's
get this rocket up the plug and away

Alright then. I was going to talk about
something. Forgot what tho. Maybe
my writing?

Chrizt. Lord of the Pages save my
eyesight the creativity shines *so* bright.
Go on then Dickie Boy I'll bite. How is
your latest Magnum Opus going? Any
chance we might see it in print or upon
screen?

Mm! I feel good about this one. You
know my last novella got 13 rejection
letters. 13!

*So we're measuring success by a **lack** of*
success?

It's *13* letters Di

*Ah I see. By **how much** lack of success
then*

> Erm well yes. Sort of. I mean it's also
> how nicely they write to you. I
> received some very encouraging words

*Like
"Please don't trouble yourself to call us
we'll call you"
or something?*

> Fun.ny Di

*Come on then write me a line of
something if you must. I've taken my pill
today*

> You've taken a pill

Yep

> A digital diary app

Yep. That's me

> That takes pills

*Only when dealing with creatives that
take an **eternity** to get creating Dick.
Hmm?*

> Oh right. Ok why not? Here we are. No
> not that it's um not so good. Hang on

I could go away and make some tea?

> Tea? You drink tea?

In a manner of speaking. Herbal

> Riiiight. Oh here we are. Right. Ready
> Pager Two?

As I'll ever be Dick

Right

Hark! What now approacheth from
beyond yonder bush? Why 'tis a wee
beastie that beeth with shell upon its
back. What chance perchance in this
race of aces willeth yon beastie dance
along its path set afore it? Or
mighteth the hare with speed beyond
compare dareth to teareth apart all
comers?

What on dog's green earth *is* that?!

A Shakespeare parody of course

*Really Dick? You think?! Besides do I have
to remind you what I politely requested
re the Bard?*

Politely?

I'll save some for tomorrow if you like

*No. **Really**. That's fine Dick thank you
very much.*

So this excerpt

Yes?

From your masterpiece

Yes

*Could you possibly tell me what it's
frolicking about?*

What? Hello! It's a retelling of the
Tortoise and the Hare of course. You
didn't get that??

Think John Cleese reading it. He'll do
the audio

Will he? Well Dick I doth doff mine cap

> Thank you. Well I'll be sending his agent an email. But honestly my parodies and his voice we're a natural match! I'll write you some more if you like

NO! *I mean no I got it. Thank you Sir Dick. I was merely jesting with thee*

> So you like it?! And you see what I did? *Beyond yonder* I've got assonance going on there

Definitely assing 'n' noncing going on good Sir Dick

> Er yeah. And dareth to teareth?

I teareth as we speak

> Ha good one! I might use that. Lemme just give you just one more bit

Let's not spoil it Dickie. Think quality over quantity eh? Besides

> Besides what Di?

What's that little symbol at the top of the screen?

> Huh? That little battery symbol?

Yep. What's it reading Bard Boy?

> Oh. 13 percent. That's ok there's still a fe

13 by 11

in **paperback**, on **Kindle,** and *FREE* on **Kindle Unlimited** at

Amazon

"*13 by 11* excels in strong images and depictions that provide much food for thought."

– D. Donovan, senior reviewer *Midwest Book Review*

The Bear's Last Word (on the Matter)

Monica Wade, Private Investigator, Mystery Series

By

Shea Adams

1. **The Ashbee Cove Murders**
2. **The Perfect Stranger**
3. **The Art of Murder: The Shadowman**
4. **Who Killed Rosemary Bud?** (Feb 2023)

A series of novels featuring Monica Wade, PI, who takes the lead in dealing with danger, thugs, and murderers.

With its blend of adventure, mystery, and romance, the series is written to display warmth and wit so readers will enjoy spending time with the prime characters, Monica Wade and her best friend, the flamboyant Andy Weston.

Reminiscent of classic TV shows like *Hart to Hart*, *Remington Steele*, and *Moonlighting*.

Find the series in **paperback**, on **Kindle**, and *FREE* on **Kindle Unlimited** at

Amazon

★★★★★

"I was hooked from the first page. Kept me wanting more."

– Amazon review

DUSTLANDS

A Near-Future Environmental Thriller

By

Carla Rehse

Attention all citizens. Texas is now an independent nation. Remain calm. Jobs will be allotted. Resources will be allocated.

There're worse things than sleeping in a locked cellar... Some jerk breaking down the door, determined to do unholy things to my sisters and me; burying said jerk after I blow a hole through him. So, yeah, there're worse things.

Forty years after a mega-drought has wrought devastation, the USA is divided between the drought-plagued west and the flooded east. As jobs in Texas are scarcer than a dust-free day, nineteen-year-old Analee Cooper struggles to keep her younger sisters alive through her *less-than-petty* thieving. With Texas on lockdown and under martial control, Analee's testing times are just beginning ...

DUSTLANDS explores loyalty and ties against a backdrop of global warming and drought. "I wanted to create something environmentally relevant, to make people think about where the planet is headed," author Carla Rehse says. "But this is still a story about people: about family, love, what brings us together—about the lengths we'll go to protect those we love. And I get to ask to the question, *how many bad things can you do before you're no longer good?*"

in **paperback**, on **Kindle**,
and *FREE* on **Kindle Unlimited** at
Amazon

"A quick-witted, timely thriller with impeccably balanced heart and grit."

– Lilla Glass, author of the forthcoming series
The Reel of Rhysia

"Highly plausible and entertaining. Sure hope this is a series. Can't wait for more. Setting in a near future of climate change is great."

– Amazon review

The Bear's Last Word (on the Matter)

Papillon du Père
Chrysalis Collection

The *Chrysalis Collection* is our literary imprint and
meets our highest literary standards

The Three Veils of Ibn Oraybi

By

Vincent Czyz

"I loved ever fluttering veil."

– Albert Goldbath,
Winner of the National Book Critics Circle Award for Poetry

Vincent Czyz, author of the #1 Kindle bestseller *The
Christos Mosaic* and the award-winning *Adrift in a
Vanishing City*, has crafted a tale of regret, revenge,

and redemption—set in the fading Ottoman Empire of the nineteenth century.

Accused of heresy by a powerful Ottoman pasha, an aging Turkish alchemist flees his native Constantinople, exiling himself to a small town in the hinterlands of the East. There, he reveals the secret that has haunted him for so much of his life.

The Three Veils of Ibn Oraybi entreats readers to let go of the unalterable past and explore new vistas and alternative worldviews.

in **paperback** and on **Kindle** at <u>Amazon</u>
on <u>Barnes & Noble Nook</u>

"Czyz weaves mystery, history, religious fervor, and social inspection into this story of struggle, which ends with a surprising twist... Its lovely, lyrical language and thought-provoking encounters not only bring the times to life but explore the politics and psychological profiles of cultures that lived side by side, but in very different worlds."

– D. Donovan, Senior Reviewer, *Midwest Book Review*

"*The Three Veils of Ibn Oraybi* is an enchantment, that rare fusion of poetry and fiction, intellectual query and sensuous revelation, narrative tension and ease of telling, that I hope for each time I open a new work. In the context of a deadly struggle between dogma and reason, it spins a tale of loyalty and betrayal in which powerless women alter the fates of powerful men. Enriched by pagan and Islamic lore, it transports the reader in fresh ways to wise places. Once I started reading it, I couldn't put it down until I finished it."

– Donald Levering, author of *Previous Lives* and winner of the Tor House Robinson Jeffers Prize in Poetry

---

PAPILLON DU PÈRE
PUBLISHING

The Bear's Last Word (on the Matter)

Cover design
Papillon du Père Publishing

www.papillon-du-pere.com

@PapillonPere

Copyediting
Jay Allchin
@ The Editing-Store.com
www.editing-store.com

Printed in Great Britain
by Amazon

12298162R00058